S0-BSQ-441

THE FROZEN RAINBOW

READ ALL OF THE ENCHANTING ADVENTURES!

The Silver Secret

The Crystal Rose

The Frozen Rainbow

The Enchanted Waterfall

SNOW SISTERS

THE FROZEN RAINBOW

By Astrid Foss
Illustrated by Monique Dong

ALADDIN
NEW YORK LONDON TORONTO SYDNEY NEW DELHI

ALADDIN
An imprint of Simon & Schuster Children's Publishing Division
1230 Avenue of the Americas, New York, New York 10020
First Aladdin hardcover edition April 2021

Originally published in Great Britain by Nosy Crow Ltd
Also available in an Aladdin paperback edition.

Jacket designed by Heather Palisi
The text of this book was set in GaramondDTInfant.
Manufactured in the United States of America 0321 FFG
2 4 6 8 10 9 7 5 3 1
Library of Congress Cataloging-in-Publication Data
Names: Foss, Astrid, author. | Dong, Monique, illustrator.
Title: The frozen rainbow / by Astrid Foss ; illustrated by Monique Dong.
Description: First Aladdin hardcover edition. | New York : Aladdin, 2021. |
Series: Snow sisters ; 3 | Audience: Grades 4-6. | Audience: Ages 7-10 |
Summary: "Three sisters with magic powers have to reach the purple Everchanging Light before it is stolen by the Shadow Witch in the third book of the Snow Sisters series"— Provided by publisher.
Identifiers: LCCN 2020018050 (print) | LCCN 2020018051 (ebook) | ISBN 9781534443549 (paperback) | ISBN 9781534443556 (hardcover) | ISBN 9781534443563 (ebook)
Subjects: CYAC: Sisters—Fiction. | Triplets—Fiction. | Magic—Fiction. | Snow—Fiction. | Fantasy.
Classification: LCC PZ7.1.F672 Fr 2021 (print) | LCC PZ7.1.F672 (ebook) | DDC [Fic]—dc23
LC record available at https://lccn.loc.gov/2020018050
LC ebook record available at https://lccn.loc.gov/2020018051

Prologue

A biting wind blew across the island of Nordovia. It swept from the jagged ice-capped mountains in the north to the snowy plains and dark pinewoods of the south. The sky was iron-gray and seemed to press down on the land. Wolves howled mournfully in the woods while Arctic foxes and hares hid in their dens, and people huddled around the fires in their cottages.

Once, Nordovia had been a glittering, happy

place, lit by the magical purple, pink, and blue Everchanging Lights that danced and swirled across the sky. But then Veronika, the Shadow Witch, had returned.

She had come back from the darkness of Svelgast Mountain to steal the Everchanging Lights. She didn't care that by taking them she would throw Nordovia into darkness and chaos, and she didn't care that, as a member of the Aurora family, it was her duty to protect the Lights and the island. She just wanted to take the Lights' magic for herself and use their great power for evil.

Her sister, Freya, had tried to stop her. She had managed to contain the Lights in three magical orbs, one purple, one pink, and one blue, and hidden them across the land using her own magical powers.

But then Veronika had imprisoned Freya

in an ice cave carved into the side of a remote mountain.

Freya lay on the floor of the cave, her face as pale as fresh snow, her long red hair tangled, her once beautiful dress torn and dirty. Over her stood the Shadow Witch, her dark cloak reaching her feet, her raven hair falling around her shoulders. She was strong and powerful, her coal-dark eyes glowing.

"You will tell me where the purple orb is, Sister!"

"Never!" Freya panted.

Veronika made a sharp twisting motion with her hands. Freya instantly cried out in pain. Her green eyes clouded over and her head slumped to the ground.

In a corner of the cave, Freya's husband, Magnus, struggled desperately against the invisible magic bonds that held him tight. "You must stop this, Veronika!" he gasped.

"Not until she tells me where the purple orb is!" Veronika snapped. "I must have it before the Day of the Midnight Sun in three days' time." She turned back to Freya, who was returning to consciousness. "Tell me where it is, Sister. It is pointless to try to fight me now that I have taken all your magic."

With a huge effort, Freya raised her head. "Not . . . quite . . . all. My daughters will find the purple orb before you. Just like they found the pink orb and the blue orb. I will do all I can to help them."

Veronika's face turned ice-hard. "Very well. If you wish to put your daughters in danger, then so be it." She gave a harsh laugh. "Just remember, you could have helped them, Freya. You could have saved them."

"I do not believe they need saving," cried Freya, a flame of defiance lighting up her emerald-green eyes as she sat up. "I think they'll stop you!"

Veronika spun around, her cloak swinging out behind her. Muttering a harsh-sounding spell, she started to change. Her shoulders stooped, her face became covered with deep wrinkles, and her hair turned gray.

"What are you doing?" Magnus demanded

A wolflike smile caught at the Shadow Witch's mouth. "I'm going to use my new magic—the magic I have taken from you—to find your precious girls," she cackled. "They will not recognize me disguised like this, and I will learn all they know about the purple orb." She shuffled to the entrance of the ice cave and moved her hand in a circle.

Moments later an enormous snow-white saber-toothed lion appeared. Throwing back his head, he opened his mouth and roared, showing off his enormous curved fangs.

Freya and Magnus exchanged horrified looks.

"The purple orb shall be mine, dear Sister!" hissed the Shadow Witch. With a triumphant laugh, she leapt onto the lion's back and galloped away.

"Magnus!" cried Freya. "We have to stop her before she gets to our girls."

"We cannot, my love," said Magnus despairingly. "All we can do is hope our daughters get the better of her and restore the Everchanging Lights to the island."

"Before it's too late," Freya whispered.

Chapter One

Hanna, Magda, and Ida Aurora were kneeling on the cozy red rug on the floor of their bedchamber in the castle. Oskar, their pet Nordovian polar bear cub, was lying beside Magda, whuffling happily as she stroked his fluffy white fur. Ida was braiding her blond hair into a single plait as Hanna talked.

"I can't wait to go to the Rainbow Pools,"

Hanna said to her sisters. "Apparently some are so hot they can boil you alive!"

Ida looked worried. "But we haven't worked out a proper plan yet. I'm really not sure about going to the Rainbow Pools today."

"We haven't got time to wait!" Hanna

protested. "It's just three days until the Day of the Midnight Sun. If we don't find the last orb by then, we won't be able to unite the Lights and get back Mother's magic. If evil Aunt Veronika gets the orb before us, we'll never free Mother and Father and save Nordovia."

"I think Hanna's right. We have to go today," said Magda, pushing her long dark-brown hair back behind her ears. The triplets all had emerald-green eyes, just like their mother, but their hair was very different. Magda's long hair was the color of dark chocolate, Hanna's hair was short and the red of autumn leaves, and Ida's was honey blond.

"Are you sure the purple orb is hidden near the Rainbow Pools, Ida?" Magda went on.

Ida nodded. "As sure as I can be. Mother told us to use the tapestry—that it would give us clues about where to look." The tapestry was a huge wall hanging showing the Nordovian flag, which hung in the hallway of the castle.

It displayed the three ancient symbols of Nordovia—a snow hawk, a crystal rose, and a perfect rainbow.

"We found the first orb near the snow hawk's

nest," Ida said. "And the second orb in the petals of a crystal rose—"

"Those adventures were so much fun!" Hanna interrupted.

Magda grinned. Hanna was right. The trips to find the first two orbs had been scary and dangerous . . . but exciting and fun, too!

"We did almost get killed," Ida pointed out.

"We got back safely in the end so it was fine," said Hanna airily.

Magda saw Ida start to frown. "So, you think the third orb will be hidden near a rainbow then, Ida?" she said quickly, wanting to head off the argument she could tell was brewing. Her two sisters were just so different!

Ida nodded. "There's a book in the library that says the best place to see rainbows is by the Rainbow Pools that lie to the east. That's where rainbows form in the mists of the hot springs.

But it will be dangerous—the springs are heated by bubbling lava!"

"So, we travel to the east today." Hanna's eyes glowed at the thought as she jumped to her feet. "I can't wait!"

"I've told you, I don't think we should." Ida faced her sister. "Not only is it dangerous, which you don't seem to care about, but the only plan you've come up with is that when Madame Olga takes us into town this morning, we run away when she's not looking, and somehow travel miles and miles to the east of the kingdom."

"Yes," said Hanna. "So?"

"That's not a plan!" Ida exclaimed. "We need to work out how we're going to get away from Madame Olga and how we're going to travel east when we do. And anyway, what about poor Madame Olga? If we do run off without telling her where we're going, she'll be beside herself with worry. I think it's stupid to rush into this."

Oskar whimpered. He didn't like it when the sisters disagreed.

"Please don't argue," Magda pleaded. "Ida, I think Hanna's right, we haven't got time to sit around and plan. Today's the only day when we will get a chance to leave the castle because of Madame Olga wanting to take us shopping for this silly ball. I agree we should plan it more but we'll just have to do that on the journey into town."

Ida bit her lip. She didn't want to argue with both her sisters. Oskar pushed his head against her leg. "Okay," she said reluctantly.

"We'll all keep thinking, and by the time we get there, maybe we will have a proper plan," said Magda, squeezing Ida's hand comfortingly.

"And if we haven't, we'll just think of something when we're there," said Hanna. "Maybe I can use my magic to make a cart fall over in front of Madame Olga, or make a clothesline snap when she's walking underneath it, and that will give us a chance to run away." She chuckled. "Just imagine Madame Olga with some big bloomers on her head!"

Even Ida had to smile at that image.

The three sisters all had their own individual magic power that had appeared on their twelfth birthday. It was because they had been born into the Aurora family—the family who were the Keepers of the Everchanging Lights. Each member of the family had a unique power, but as they got older they could learn to use other types of magic, just like Freya and Veronika had done. Hanna's magic let her move objects around with her mind. Ida could draw an object and make it come to life, and Magda could turn into any animal she saw.

"Madame Olga will be calling us soon," said Hanna. "Have we got everything we talked about? Have you got the map of Nordovia, Ida?"

"Yes, it's in the pocket of my traveling cloak," said Ida. "And I've got my sketchbook and pencils, too."

"I've got some food," said Magda, going over to her bed and pulling a leather bag out from underneath it. "I disguised myself as a butterfly and flew into the kitchen this morning. I waited until cook was out of the way, then I turned back into myself and filled this bag with bread, cheese, apples, and dried fruit."

"That was really good thinking," said Ida. "Well done."

"Well, yesterday, I used my magic to make a compass fly off the shelf in Madame Olga's room

M

and come to my hand," said Hanna quickly. She pulled the compass out of her pocket. "This will help us find the way, and I'll put it back as soon we get home. It'll be really useful, won't it?"

"It will," Ida agreed. She hid a small smile. Her sisters could be very competitive!

Magda walked over to a delicate wooden table in the center of the room, where a large and beautiful snow globe stood. Inside the globe, soft snowflakes fell around a waterfall that tumbled down a tall cliff into an icy sea. Pink and blue lights swirled through the snowflakes. When the sisters had found the blue and pink orbs, they had taken them to the snow globe and the Lights had been absorbed inside. They were safe there—at least until the Day of the Midnight Sun, the most magical day of the year, when the sun never set.

Looking at the pink and blue lights, Magda

felt determination rush through her. "We must find the purple orb today," she said.

"And then we can free Mother and Father and defeat Aunt Veronika!" said Hanna.

Sensing their excitement, Oskar gave a yip and gamboled around their legs. He tumbled onto his back, asking for his tummy to be tickled. Magda and Hanna giggled and bent to stroke him, but Ida was distracted by the globe.

"Look at the snowflakes!" she exclaimed. "They're doing something strange."

The snowflakes were swirling faster inside the glass.

"Do you think Mother's trying to talk to us?" Magda breathed.

A couple of times, their mother had been able to use what remained of her powers to talk to the girls through the snow globe.

"Oh, I hope she is!" said Ida longingly. They all missed their mother and father so much.

Hanna searched the snowflakes, hoping to see their mother's face and loving green eyes, but no image appeared. "There's nothing there," she said in disappointment.

"Listen," said Magda. She put her finger to her lips and they all listened hard. A weak voice whispered through the room.

"My darling girls . . . Can you hear me?"

"Mother!" the triplets cried.

Freya's words came in short bursts. "I am weak. Your aunt has taken most of my magic now, and I'm using the last of my powers to send this message. Find the frozen rainbow . . ."

"The frozen rainbow?" echoed Hanna. "How can a rainbow be frozen?"

"Hanna! Shush!" said Ida.

There was a pause and then they heard their mother take a rasping breath. "You must go to the Rainbow Pools. But watch out for a stranger. Beware . . ." Her faint words faded.

"Mother!" said Ida desperately.

But there was no reply.

The girls looked at one another.

"What did she mean?" Magda said, breaking the tense silence.

"I've no idea," said Hanna slowly. "Who's this stranger we have to beware of? And what was she saying about a frozen rainbow?" She looked at Ida. "Can rainbows freeze?"

Ida looked confused. "I don't know. I've never read about frozen rainbows." She felt her eyes fill with tears. It had been so hard to hear their mother's voice and know that the Shadow Witch was hurting her. She swallowed hard. Crying wouldn't help. "We have to go," she said suddenly. "You're right, Hanna. We must head east today. We have to stop Aunt Veronika."

Hanna reached out and took her sisters' hands. "We can do this," she said. "We can find the purple orb and save Mother and Father—and Nordovia!"

Chapter Two

Shining white snow crystals flew up from the four ponies' hooves as they pulled the sleigh. They were heading toward the nearby town, with the driver, Lars, urging them on. The girls huddled together under thick woolen blankets, their bags for the journey ahead hidden by their feet, their cheeks stinging. It was always cold in Nordovia, but since the Everchanging Lights had faded, the air had seemed even icier. Oskar was curled up under the blankets with them, like a furry hot-water bottle. Nordovian polar bears were magical and they could change size, growing really big when they wanted to. At that moment Oskar was cub-size.

Madame Olga, their governess, sat opposite them, a notebook in her hand as she went through her list of things to do in town. Her hair was pulled back in a tidy roll at the

base of her neck, her scarf arranged neatly, and her coat buttoned up to the top.

The jingle of the bells on the harness and the swish of the sleigh's runners through the thick snow broke the silence. All the birds and animals seemed to have gone into hiding. The gray sky looked heavy, with an occasional faint hint of pale blue, purple, and pink flickering across it.

Magda looked around anxiously. Nordovia was usually such a beautiful place, full of life and light, but now it seemed so dull and sad. They had to help save the land—she couldn't bear it if they failed.

Madame Olga looked up. "We'll be in town very soon, girls. When we are there, may I remind you that it is of the utmost importance that you appear to be in good spirits. The people are unhappy and afraid and they will look to you. If they see you looking miserable, then it will not help morale. While we are in town we will shop for items that are needed for the forthcoming ball on the Day of the Midnight Sun."

"I can't believe people are still planning for the ball to go ahead!" Hanna burst out. "We shouldn't be having a ball when Mother and Father are missing. It's wrong, Madame Olga!"

Madame Olga gave her a sharp look. "Hanna Aurora, that is not the way young ladies should speak to their elders. Have I taught you nothing?" Hanna's face fell and Madame Olga's expression softened. "I do understand your feelings, my dear," she said, leaning forward, "but we must be brave. We must carry on as normal and you must uphold the Aurora family's responsibilities. You will have to stand in for your parents and host the ball."

Ida gulped. "Do we really have to?" She hated the thought of hosting the celebration feast and ball and having everyone looking at them. It felt so wrong to be taking their parents' place.

"You do," said Madame Olga firmly. She looked at the three girls' glum faces. "Come, my dears, the guards are scouring the country. There may yet be good news—your parents may be rescued by the time of the celebrations. We are all hoping that that will be the case."

Hanna, Magda, and Ida exchanged looks. The adults might think they were going to be able to find and free Freya and Magnus, but the girls knew that the only chance they had of rescuing them was to find the orb and fight the Shadow Witch with magic. The guards could not do that—only they could.

It's all down to us, Magda thought.

She put her hand on Oskar's head, and he licked her with his rough tongue and whuffled. *And me*, he seemed to be saying.

Magda smiled. Oskar had definitely helped in their first two adventures; maybe he would help them again this time.

The ponies cantered out of the trees, and the girls saw the town ahead of them, with its wooden buildings and narrow streets.

"Here we are," said Madame Olga. "Smile please, girls, and be on your best behavior."

Once in town, the girls got out of the sleigh, carefully hiding their bags under their cloaks, and headed down the main street with Madame Olga and Oskar. People were bustling about with shopping baskets, hurrying in and out of the brightly lit shops and stopping at the market stalls to buy food and to chat to the traders. The smell of frying sausages and roasting chestnuts filled the air. There were carts laden with mountains of fresh fruit and vegetables, tables groaning with large round cheeses, and stalls selling woolen scarves and socks and pretty jewelry.

The girls kept their heads high and smiled at everyone they passed. The people smiled back, but Ida saw them whispering behind their hands.

"It's the Aurora girls," Ida heard one woman

saying. "Look at them, the poor things. They must be worried sick about their parents."

"Has there been any news?"

"No, none."

Ida tried to shut her ears to the whispers. Madame Olga stopped to inspect some jewelry at a market stall. Magda and Hanna went to pet a sturdy brown pony who was tied to a post and Ida made her way to a market stall selling secondhand books.

She was browsing through the titles when she felt a prickling across her shoulders and had the strangest feeling that someone was watching her. She swung around and saw an old lady bundled up in lots of layers standing in the shadows. Her coal-black eyes were sharp in her wrinkled face as she stared intently at Ida. For a moment, Ida was reminded of a wolf staring hungrily at its prey.

An icy shiver ran down Ida's spine and she backed away. She hurried to join Madame Olga. When she reached her, she glanced back, but the old woman had vanished, leaving just a dark patch of empty shadow.

Ida blinked. Where had she gone? She couldn't just have disappeared!

"Hanna! Magda! We must go to the haberdasher's, girls!" said Madame Olga, sweeping toward a nearby shop selling material and ribbon.

Ida followed her, glancing back at the shadows as she did so. She wondered whether she should say something to her sisters, but decided not to. It was probably nothing and she didn't want to seem scared and silly.

The shop assistant, a lady about the same age as Madame Olga, was talking anxiously to a customer. "It's a dreadful situation," she was saying in hushed tones. "I heard the Shadow Witch is back." She shivered.

"Whatever are we going to do?" said the customer fearfully. "What if Magnus and Freya never return?"

As the girls and their governess entered, they broke off.

"Madame Olga!" The shop assistant curtseyed. "And the three young Auroras. I am honored indeed."

The customer quickly hurried out of the shop.

"How may I help you?" the assistant asked.

"We need ribbons for the girls' hair for the ball, Helga," said Madame Olga. "Now, let me see. I wonder which colors will suit them best?"

The girls had to stand patiently while Madame Olga held up lengths of differently colored ribbon to their hair. Hanna wanted to scream with frustration. She fidgeted impatiently and received a sharp look from Madame Olga. Oskar soon got bored and curled up into a ball in a basket of scrap materials and went to sleep, his black nose tucked against his stumpy white tail.

It seemed to take forever, but finally the girls' ribbons had been decided—green for Hanna, blue for Ida, and purple for Magda.

Madame Olga's eyes fell on a display of bonnets. "Those bonnets look well made," she said approvingly.

"Oh, they are, Madame Olga," said the assistant. "Would you like to try one on? The dark red would look most fetching against your hair."

Madame Olga nodded. "Maybe I will."

Hanna groaned inwardly. Time was passing. They really needed to get out of the shop and escape! But how? There was no way Madame Olga was going to let them go outside on their own. They needed a distraction. Her eyes glanced to where three hat stands were lined up side by side, displaying a selection of winter hats. If one of the hat stands fell over, then it would knock into the next hat stand, and then the next. Maybe this was their chance!

"I like this hat over here," she said, stepping toward the nearest hat stand. "Why don't you try this one on, Madame Olga?"

Hanna saw Magda and Ida's puzzled looks and winked at them, hoping they would guess she had a plan. As she reached the hat stand she pretended to stumble.

"Oh goodness!" she gasped, reaching out with her hands as she fell into the hat stand. It crashed down into the next hat stand, which also toppled over with a bang. Hats and bonnets flew everywhere, helped by a little of Hanna's magic!

Madame Olga shrieked, and staggered back, falling over as hats rained down on her.

The shop assistant gasped. "Oh, Madame Olga, let me help you," she said, rushing to her assistance.

"Quick!" Hanna whispered to her sisters. "This is our chance!"

Grabbing their hands, she pulled them out of the shop. It was time for their adventure to begin!

Chapter Three

"We've escaped!" exclaimed Magda as they rushed out into the busy street. "What now, though? How do we get to the east?"

Ida glanced back anxiously to where Madame Olga was being helped to her feet. "Madame Olga's going to be worried sick if we just disappear. Can't we leave her a note or something?"

"No, if we tell her where we're going, she'll come after us." Hanna glanced around. Her eyes fell on the pony that she and Magda had been patting earlier.

"I know!" she said. "We'll use the pony over there!"

"We can't all ride one pony," Magda pointed out.

"No, but if Ida uses her magic to draw a sleigh and a harness then he'll be able to pull us through the snow." Hanna turned to Ida. "Can you do that, Ida?"

Ida nodded. Crouching down, she grabbed a stick from the ground and began to sketch a picture of a sleigh and harness in the trampled-down snow beside him. Magic tingled through her fingers as she drew.

"You're coming on an adventure with us," Magda murmured, stroking the pony. He nuzzled her hands. She saw a name tag on his halter that said CASPAR.

"Quickly, Ida!" Hanna urged, glancing back at the shop. Madame Olga was looking around, her eyes widening as she realized the girls were no longer there.

"Done it!" said Ida. The lines of the drawing seemed to shiver, and then suddenly they vanished, and a real sleigh with green sides, red runners, and a red seat just big enough for three people was in the snow next to them. The pony jumped in surprise and snorted.

"Steady, Caspar," Magda soothed. "It's all right. Don't worry. There's nothing to be scared of."

The pony's ears flickered as he listened to her voice. Calming down, he let Magda start attaching the harness to him. She worked quickly, hoping his owner wouldn't appear and ask what they were doing!

Hanna saw Madame Olga say something to the assistant and head for the door of the shop. She was about to come out! *I've got to stop her*, Hanna thought.

Her eyes fell on a barrel of apples near the shop door. Concentrating hard, she felt magic surge through her. She grinned as she used the power to move the barrel with her mind, pushing it up against the shop door and barricading Madame

Olga inside. It was getting easier to do magic now. At first she had found it hard, but now she just had to think what she wanted and it happened.

Madame Olga turned the handle of the door and tried to open it. Hanna saw the surprise on her face as she peered through the glass and spotted the barrel blocking her way.

"We've got to go right now!" she said urgently.

"We're ready!" said Magda, fastening the last buckle and jumping into the sleigh. "Jump on board!" She flicked the reins. "Let's go!" she cried to Caspar the pony.

He leapt forward. Hanna jumped onto the sleigh and grabbed Ida's hands, pulling her on too. They held on to the sides as the pony started

to canter haphazardly through the streets.

"Coming through!" shouted Magda as people started to jump out of the way. Chickens squawked, dogs barked, and people yelled.

"Watch out!" cried a fruit stallholder as the pony careered around her cart and knocked over a barrel of pears.

Magda grappled with the reins, trying to get

control of Caspar. "Whoa there!" she gasped. "Steady, boy!"

Caspar slowed down to a trot and Magda got full control of the reins. She used them to guide the pony around the remaining stalls and head toward the town gates. The old lady Ida had seen earlier was shuffling down the road, her dark cloak pulled around her.

"We've done it!" whooped Hanna, glancing behind at the people staring after them with astounded looks on their faces. "To the east! Rainbow Pools, here we come!"

A cackle of laughter cut across her words as the old lady swung around, sweeping off her cloak and transforming into the tall figure of their aunt, her white hair becoming midnight black and her wrinkles fading.

Caspar shied and stopped, almost overturning the sleigh. Behind them the girls could hear the townspeople crying out and shouting as they all recognized the Shadow Witch.

"Aunt Veronika!" the three girls gasped.

"Yes," their evil aunt hissed, her eyes glittering. "And thanks to your foolishness, I now know where to go. I shall travel to the Rainbow Pools and find the purple orb. I will have the power of the purple Everchanging Light!" She shrieked with glee as she saw the shock and dismay on their faces.

Hanna felt dreadful. Why had she said where they were going out loud? "You won't get to the orb before us!" she exclaimed. "We'll stop you!"

"I think not!" The Shadow Witch clapped her hands and there was a loud roar from the direction of the town gates.

"What's that?" said Ida.

The Shadow Witch's lips curved into a smile. "That, my meddling nieces, is how I shall be getting to the purple orb." As she spoke, a gigantic white lion with long curving saber-like teeth came bounding through the gates.

Caspar neighed in fear and tried to turn and gallop in the other direction. The townspeople

yelled and started to run away. "Whoa!" gasped Magda, holding on tight to the reins and just about managing to stop the terrified pony.

The lion reached the Shadow Witch and crouched down. She wrapped her hands in its thick white mane and climbed onto its back.

"Goodbye, nieces!" she hissed. "You can bid farewell to your foolish plans to save Nordovia now. The power of the Everchanging Lights will be mine!" She kicked her heels to the lion's sides and it set off, its muscles strong and powerful as it bounded through the gates.

"Quickly!" cried Hanna. "We can't let her beat us!"

"Go, Caspar!" cried Magda desperately. The pony leapt forward. The race to the Rainbow Pools had begun!

Chapter Four

Caspar raced across the snowy plains outside the town, with Magda sitting between her sisters and urging him on with shakes of the reins. Aunt Veronika's saber-toothed snow lion had already vanished from sight.

"It's so cold!" Hanna said, her teeth chattering.

Ida pulled out her sketchbook and quickly sketched some blankets. The magic tingled through her, and they appeared on the floor of the sleigh. She grabbed them before they could bounce out, and handed one to Hanna, tucking another around Magda's legs.

"Oh no!" Magda cried.

"What?" demanded Ida.

"Oskar! He's still with Madame Olga!"

The triplets looked at one another in dismay. They had been so focused on escaping from Madame Olga and heading north, they had forgotten all about Oskar.

Magda swallowed. "He was asleep in the shop when we left it. I can't believe we've come without him."

Ida bit her lip. The bear cub usually went everywhere with them. "He'll miss us so much."

"And we'll miss him," said Hanna. For once even her enthusiasm seemed dampened. "He helped us so much in the other adventures."

Magda had to fight back her tears. She hated the thought of being without Oskar. She longed to turn around and get him, but she knew they couldn't. *Oh, Oskar*, she thought. *I'm sorry*.

None of them spoke for a while. Caspar galloped on, pulling the sleigh across the snow, heading for a forest of dark pine trees with icicles hanging from every branch. The girls were lost in their own thoughts.

As they drew close to the trees, Hanna pulled the compass from her pocket and checked it.

"We need to go straight through these trees," she said, breaking the silence.

Magda could tell Caspar was tiring, his neck was foaming with sweat and his nostrils were flaring. "We need to slow down for a while," she said as they entered the gloomy woods. "Caspar needs to rest. Whoa, boy!" she called.

Caspar slowed to a trot and then a walk.

Frustration rushed through Hanna. She didn't want to slow down. Their aunt was already far ahead of them. She couldn't be allowed to reach the purple orb before them. Hanna felt a sharp flicker of guilt. Oh, why had she said out loud that they were heading for the Rainbow Pools? "We can't slow down too much," she said.

"We have to, Hanna. It's not fair to Caspar," Magda insisted.

"We should have taken two ponies," said Ida. "They could have shared the load and we would have been able to travel farther without taking a break."

"Well, maybe one of you should have thought about that before we left!" said Hanna.

"I was busy drawing the sleigh," said Ida.

"And I was calming Caspar down and harnessing him up," said Magda.

"Oh, so I should have thought of it, should I?" huffed Hanna. "It's my fault, just like everything else I suppose!"

"Well, maybe if you hadn't yelled out where we were going then we wouldn't be in such a rush," said Magda.

"And if we'd taken time to plan things, we'd have remembered to make sure we brought Oskar with us," said Ida.

"If we'd listened to you, we wouldn't be doing anything right now!" snapped Hanna. "We'd just be stuck back in the castle staring at the walls for yet another day. At least we're on our way to find the orb thanks to me."

"Oh, it's all thanks to you, is it? Well—" Ida broke off with a gasp as they rounded a corner and they saw their Aunt Veronika standing in the middle of the track. Beside her was the gigantic white saber-toothed lion.

Caspar stopped dead. Aunt Veronika hissed a word to the lion, and throwing back its head, it roared so loudly that the woods seemed to shake and snow fell from the nearby trees.

Caspar reared in terror, upsetting the sleigh and sending the girls tumbling onto the path. The lion bounded toward them. The pony turned and bolted through the trees, heading back the way they had come, the sleigh bouncing behind him. The lion stopped with a victorious snarl, and the Shadow Witch shrieked with laughter.

"So much for you getting to the east, nieces!" she cried. "You shall go no farther!"

"That's what you think!" cried Hanna, sitting up. She fixed her eyes on some icicles hanging above their aunt's head and used her magic to loosen them. CRACK! They broke off and fell down through the air like daggers. But the Shadow Witch was too quick. She clicked her fingers and the icicles exploded into millions of tiny shards.

"You think your puny magic can possibly be a match for mine?" she snapped. "If you think that, you are even more stupid than I thought!" She pointed her hand at Hanna.

Magda wasn't sure what their aunt was intending to do, but she wasn't going to wait to find out. Fixing her eyes on the saber-toothed lion, she let her magic rush through her. She felt her body changing, arms becoming legs, hands becoming paws with sharp claws, her body transforming into another lion, just as large and with just as sharp teeth. Suddenly she saw the world through the lion's eyes. She could see with incredible clarity every leaf, every pine needle, every tree root. She felt the urge to chase and hunt. Throwing back her head, she roared and then pounced.

The Shadow Witch screamed out a spell. As Magda leapt through the air, she felt her magic drain from her and she landed in a heap on the floor, just a girl once again.

The Shadow Witch swung around to where Ida was quickly drawing a picture of a net, and threw an orange fireball at her notebook. It exploded into flames. Ida staggered back clutching her burnt fingers.

"This ends now!" hissed their aunt. Her hands lifted toward the sky and she chanted a spell. Bringing her hands down, she fired three green balls of magic at the girls. The last thing they knew was the feeling of spells exploding around them, and then the world went black.

Chapter Five

Hanna was the first to wake up. Her eyes blinked open. She was lying on a freezing rocky floor. It was dark and gloomy and she ached all over. The cold seemed to bite into her face. Where was she? What was going on? Where were her sisters?

Images flashed through her mind—escaping from the town, galloping across the plains, entering the woods, them arguing, and then Aunt Veronika . . .

She tried to stand up, and only then realized her hands were tied behind her back. Wriggling onto her side, she managed to sit. She saw Magda and Ida lying on the floor nearby. For a moment her heart stopped. Were they dead? But then she saw their sides rising and falling with their breathing. Thank goodness. She glanced around. They were in a cave. An enormous boulder of ice had been rolled across the entrance, blocking the way out. Hanna got to her feet and walked unsteadily toward it. She was shivering with cold and her stomach was growling hungrily.

Hanna leaned against the ice boulder to see if it would move, but it didn't shift. *I could use my magic to move it*, she realized.

Taking a breath, she fixed her eyes on the boulder. *Move*, she thought. But nothing happened. Hanna gritted her teeth and tried again, but it was as though something more powerful than her own magic was holding the ice in place.

She cried out in frustration. Aunt Veronika must have used magic to fix it there—magic that was stronger than Hanna's own. Despair swept through her. Now what were they going to do?

She heard a small groan behind her and swung around. Ida and Magda were both starting to sit up. They were blinking dazedly. Hanna hurried over to them.

"What's . . . What's going on?" said Magda.

"Where are we?" asked Ida. She struggled. "Why are we tied up?"

"Aunt Veronika did it," Hanna said heavily.

She sat down beside her sisters and told them what had just happened. "She must have tied us up, dragged us in here, and blocked the cave entrance with ice. We're trapped. I've tried to move the ice, but I think Aunt Veronika has placed a spell that stops my magic from moving it."

"And I can't draw anything with my hands tied up," said Ida.

"And there are no animals for me to turn into," said Magda. "We really are trapped here." She shivered. "It's so cold. We're going to freeze to death."

"Or starve," said Ida.

Even Hanna couldn't find anything positive to say. She shuffled closer to her sisters. "We can't do anything about being hungry, but we can keep each other warm," she said.

They huddled together in the dark.

"I'm sorry we argued earlier," said Ida shakily.

"Me too," said Hanna, glancing apologetically at her sisters. "And I'm sorry I was the one who told Aunt Veronika where we were going."

"You didn't mean to," said Magda. "You

couldn't have known she would be there in disguise!"

"I should have said something to you both," admitted Ida. "I saw her earlier in the market and I knew there was something strange about her." She hung her head. "I'm sorry," she whispered. "I should have worked it out and told you both. Mother told us to beware of a stranger. If it's anyone's fault, it's mine, not yours, Hanna."

"You couldn't have guessed that old lady was Aunt Veronika," said Hanna. "And if we'd had a proper plan like you'd wanted, then maybe none of it would have happened and we'd be safely on our way by now."

They bent their heads together—red touching brown touching blond.

"I wouldn't like to be on my own in here," said Magda, shivering. "I'm glad we're together."

Her sisters nodded in agreement.

Suddenly, there was a snuffling, scrabbling noise at the entrance to the cave. "What's that?" said Ida in alarm.

The scrabbling got louder.

"It's an animal!" said Magda. "It's trying to get through the ice into the cave."

"What sort of animal?" said Hanna in alarm. "And why's it trying to get in?"

"Do you think it's something sent by Aunt Veronika?" Ida said, her eyes widening.

They edged cautiously to the entrance. The scrabbling got louder and then they heard a whining. What was going on? The girls gasped as a white hairy foot with long sharp claws appeared through the ice. Then another paw appeared and a familiar head with soft brown eyes poked through.

"Oskar!" the girls cried in amazement. The polar bear had used his strong claws to carve

a narrow tunnel through the block of ice. His eyes lit up as he saw them and he scrabbled through the ice, before collapsing exhausted on the cave floor.

"Oskar, you followed us!" said Magda. "You tracked the sleigh!"

Oskar whimpered as if asking them why they weren't stroking and fussing over him.

"We can't pat you, Oskar," said Ida, half turning to show him her hands tied behind her back.

Oskar heaved himself to his feet and shuffled around behind her. She felt his damp nose on her wrists as he snuffled at the ropes and then she felt a strange gnawing sensation. "He's chewing through the ropes!" she said. "If he frees me, I can draw some scissors and cut your ropes off."

The others looked at her in excitement. "And then we can escape through the tunnel he made!" said Hanna.

"Go on, Oskar," Magda encouraged. "Good boy!"

The cub chewed even harder, being careful not to graze Ida's skin with his strong teeth. She felt one rope snap, then the other, and finally her hands were free.

"Oh, thank you, Oskar!" she gasped. She rubbed her wrists. They felt numb at first, but as she moved them they started to hurt and ache. Ida ignored the pain. Pulling out her sketchbook, she drew some scissors. They appeared beside her, and she picked them up with her trembling fingers. Oskar was already chewing through Magda's ropes. Ida carefully cut Hanna free.

"Ow!" her sisters said as they rubbed their sore wrists and hands and shook the stiffness from their arms and shoulders.

Magda scooped Oskar up and kissed his soft head. "Oh, Oskar, you're amazing. Without you, we would have been trapped here forever!"

The polar bear cub made a contented whuffling noise.

"Let's get out of here," said Hanna.

Bending down, they squeezed through the tunnel Oskar had made in the block of ice, and emerged shivering into the forest.

Hanna spotted the blankets and bags that had fallen from the sleigh when it had overturned. She ran over and picked them up. "We've still got these."

"There's food in my bag," said Magda. "Let's eat. I'm starving."

"I'll magic up a fire to keep us warm," said Ida.

Soon the three girls were sitting around the blazing fire, sharing the bread and cheese and apples, and feeding Oskar bits of dried meat. With the blankets around their shoulders and the fire warming their faces, they soon stopped

shivering. The sky was dark now, and through the tree canopy they could see the faint glimmer of the moon.

"We've got to decide what

we're going to do now," said Magda. "Do we carry on or go home?"

"We've got to go on," said Ida.

"Definitely!" exclaimed Hanna. "We can't give up now. Even if Aunt Veronika did get to the Rainbow Pools, she might not have found the orb yet. The blue and pink orbs were really well hidden, so hopefully the purple orb is hidden too. And, remember, she doesn't know she's looking for a frozen rainbow."

"Whatever that means," said Ida.

"You're right. We have to go on," said Magda, remembering how weak their mother had sounded. "We can't just sit back and let Aunt Veronika win. We're Auroras. If there's still a chance we can stop her, we have to try."

Ida got to her feet. "What are we waiting for? Let's go!"

Chapter Six

Oskar grew to full size and the girls climbed onto his back. They'd done this once before, on their last adventure. Hanna clung to the thick fur at the back of his neck while Ida and Magda hung on behind her. Riding a polar bear was nothing like riding a pony; Oskar rolled from side to side, and they had to hold on tightly! As they came out of the trees onto the plains, the moon shone down, lighting their way. It was so close to the Day of the Midnight Sun—the girls knew that night would only be an hour or so long.

Oskar galloped over the plains and across the icy tundra, heading toward the snowcapped volcanic mountains that loomed in front of them. As they drew closer, they could see steam rising from the land in great white clouds. "Those must be the lava fields!" cried Ida.

"The snow's thinner here," Hanna pointed out.

"It's because it's warmer at the base of the volcanoes," said Ida. "Underneath this rock there's a sea of boiling magma—the fiery liquid that pours out when the volcano erupts. It heats the hot springs and mud pools, and creates the geysers that shoot water into the sky."

"I hope the volcano doesn't erupt today," said Magda with a shiver.

The sun had already started to rise over the horizon like a golden eye, its rays lighting up the black sky with streaks of pale gray.

Oskar reached the edge of the lava fields and stopped.

"What a strange, strange place," breathed Hanna.

In front of them, gray rock covered the land in weird ripples and waves where lava flows had cooled in the icy air. The snow barely covered it. Everywhere they looked there were steaming pools of bubbling water and craters filled with gurgling pale-blue mud. Geysers shot jets of scalding hot water high into the sky like strange fountains, and gas streamed out of holes in the rocky ground. Clouds of steam floated across the landscape.

The girls slid off Oskar's back.

"You can turn back to your usual size now,"

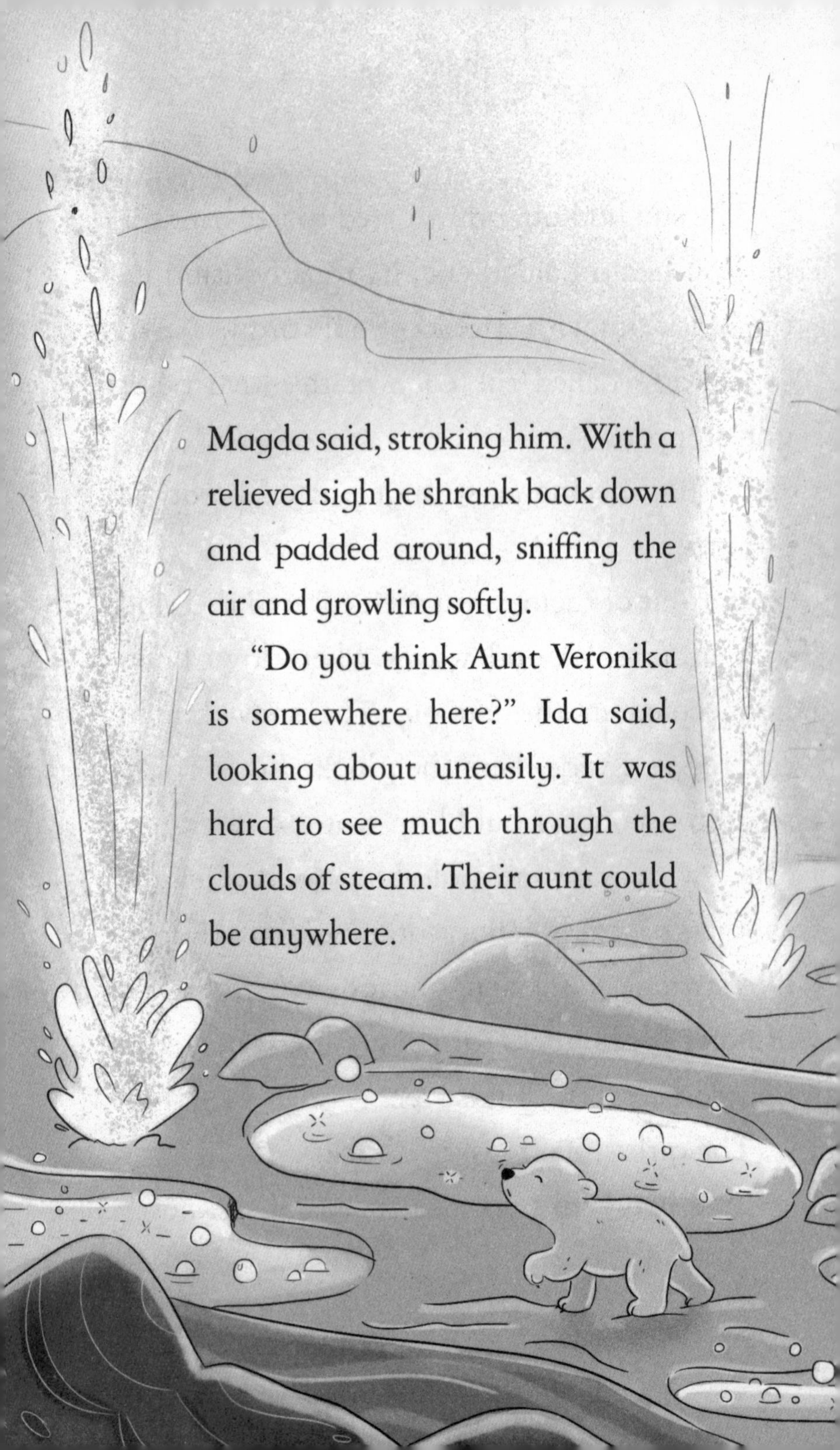

Magda said, stroking him. With a relieved sigh he shrank back down and padded around, sniffing the air and growling softly.

"Do you think Aunt Veronika is somewhere here?" Ida said, looking about uneasily. It was hard to see much through the clouds of steam. Their aunt could be anywhere.

"I wonder if she's found the orb yet," said Hanna.

"She might be here, so we'd better be really careful," said Magda. "I wonder where the Rainbow Pools are? I can't see any rainbows anywhere."

"Maybe it has to be daytime before the rainbows appear," said Ida. "A book I read in the castle library said the Rainbow Pools are at the base of the volcano."

"Let's head over there then," said Hanna. She hurried forward, but stopped with a cry as a column of boiling water and steam shot up directly in front of her. Magda and Ida pulled her back to safety as the water column disappeared back down into the ground.

"We're going to have to go slowly!" Ida said, her heart beating fast. "There are all sorts of dangers here. Not just the geysers shooting hot water up, but the boiling pools of mud. And even the pools that aren't boiling have such thick mud that they could suck us down into their depths."

"We'll go very slowly," said Magda. "Won't we, Hanna?" She held on to her sister's arm, knowing how impatient she could be.

"All right," Hanna agreed reluctantly.

"And keep our eyes peeled for Aunt Veronika," warned Magda. "Remember, she could be anywhere."

They set off cautiously across the lava fields, Oskar bounding along beside the girls.

The rocky ground rose up and down, and they had to skirt around the treacherous mud pools and geysers, being very careful not to slip into any of them while keeping alert for any sign of their aunt. They made very slow progress.

Magda watched the sun rising in the sky and thought of Madame Olga. She would be so worried about them. She wished they could go faster, but she knew it wouldn't be safe.

"If only we knew where Aunt Veronika is," Hanna said. "I keep thinking she's going to appear at any moment."

"Or that the lion is going to pounce on us," agreed Ida.

"Maybe I can use my magic to work out where they are," said Magda, looking thoughtfully at a family of white Arctic hares who were playing on a patch of short grass just ahead of them. When they had been searching for the blue orb she had transformed into an Arctic fox. She could still remember how vivid the smells had been and how clear her eyesight had become when she had been a fox. Maybe if she turned into a hare, the same thing would happen? "If I turn into an Arctic hare, I might be able to track down Aunt Veronika."

Hanna nodded. "Good idea. We'll be able to go faster if we're not having to watch out for her with every step."

"Be careful, though," said Ida.

Magda fixed her eyes on the hares and let the rest of the world fade away. She imagined having four paws, sensitive ears, and a twitching nose. Magic rushed into her, and she felt herself starting to shrink. Suddenly she realized she was staring at Hanna and Ida's knees. She blinked and gazed around. The world looked

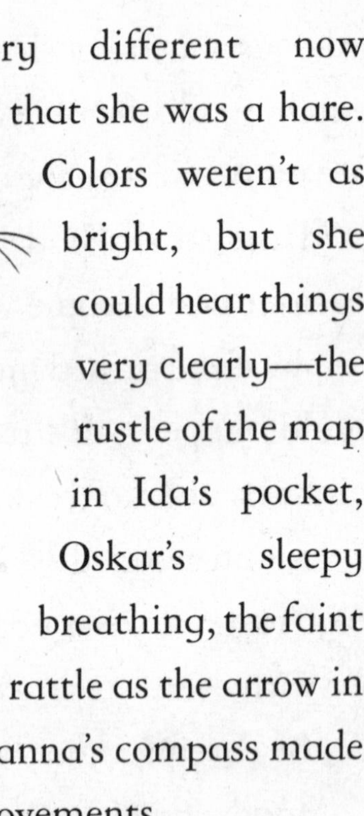

very different now that she was a hare. Colors weren't as bright, but she could hear things very clearly—the rustle of the map in Ida's pocket, Oskar's sleepy breathing, the faint rattle as the arrow in Hanna's compass made tiny movements.

She sat up on her hind legs and sniffed the air. Beneath the overwhelming egglike stench of the mud, she could catch the smell of the other hares and her sisters' unique scents—Hanna smelling like fresh grass and Ida smelling of rose petals. She could also sense something else, a faint scent coming from the base of the volcano. She felt her whiskers twitching in alarm. It was something to be scared of, something large and fierce that made her want to bolt into a hole. She realized what it was—the white lion!

Magda fought back her fear and headed toward the scent. She knew she would have to be careful. If the lion saw her, he'd probably eat her in one gulp! She hopped past steaming pools and craters filled with blue-gray mud. To her relief, she no longer had to think which was the safe way to go, an animal instinct for danger guided her nimble paws. She stopped as a cloud of steam cleared and she saw an amazing sight in front of her—at least thirty geysers randomly shooting columns of steam and water up into the sky at the foot of the volcano. The sun was shining down and

rainbows were forming over the geysers into shimmering arches of multicolored light. She'd found the Rainbow Pools!

She spotted a tall figure with long dark hair standing some way off beside the saber-toothed lion and she pressed

herself to the ground, her whiskers twitching frantically. She'd also found Aunt Veronika!

Every instinct in her hare

body told her to turn and run, but she forced herself not to give in. Heart pounding, she hopped closer.

Her aunt didn't notice. Her eyes were fixed on the columns of steam and she was muttering to herself.

"It's got to be here somewhere, but where?" the Shadow Witch was snarling. "I must find it."

Magda felt a rush of relief. Aunt Veronika hadn't found the orb yet! That meant they still had a chance to save Nordovia and their parents.

The Shadow Witch tossed back her hair and raised a hand to the sky. She called out a string of harsh words. Lightning flashed from her fingers but then sizzled to the ground and went out. She stamped her foot in frustration. "Why is my magic not finding it?" she screamed.

Magda hopped away. Now she knew where Aunt Veronika was she could warn the others.

She raced back across the lava fields to where Ida and Hanna were waiting. Reaching them, she transformed back into herself.

"What happened? Did you find the frozen rainbow?" demanded Ida.

Magda shook her head, gasping for breath and pointing back to where she had come from. "No, but I've found Aunt Veronika. She's over there!"

"But where's the orb?" Hanna cried in frustration, stamping her foot.

"Let me think," said Ida slowly. "There was something in the book I read about one geyser set apart from the others that shoots into the sky so often that it appears to always have a rainbow over it. Maybe we need to look for that geyser."

She scanned the landscape and noticed something—in the opposite direction of where

Magda had seen Aunt Veronika. The sky looked slightly different. It was a paler blue with a slight lilac tint. Ida watched two birds that had been flying in a straight line toward the paler sky suddenly bank and swoop around it. That was odd.

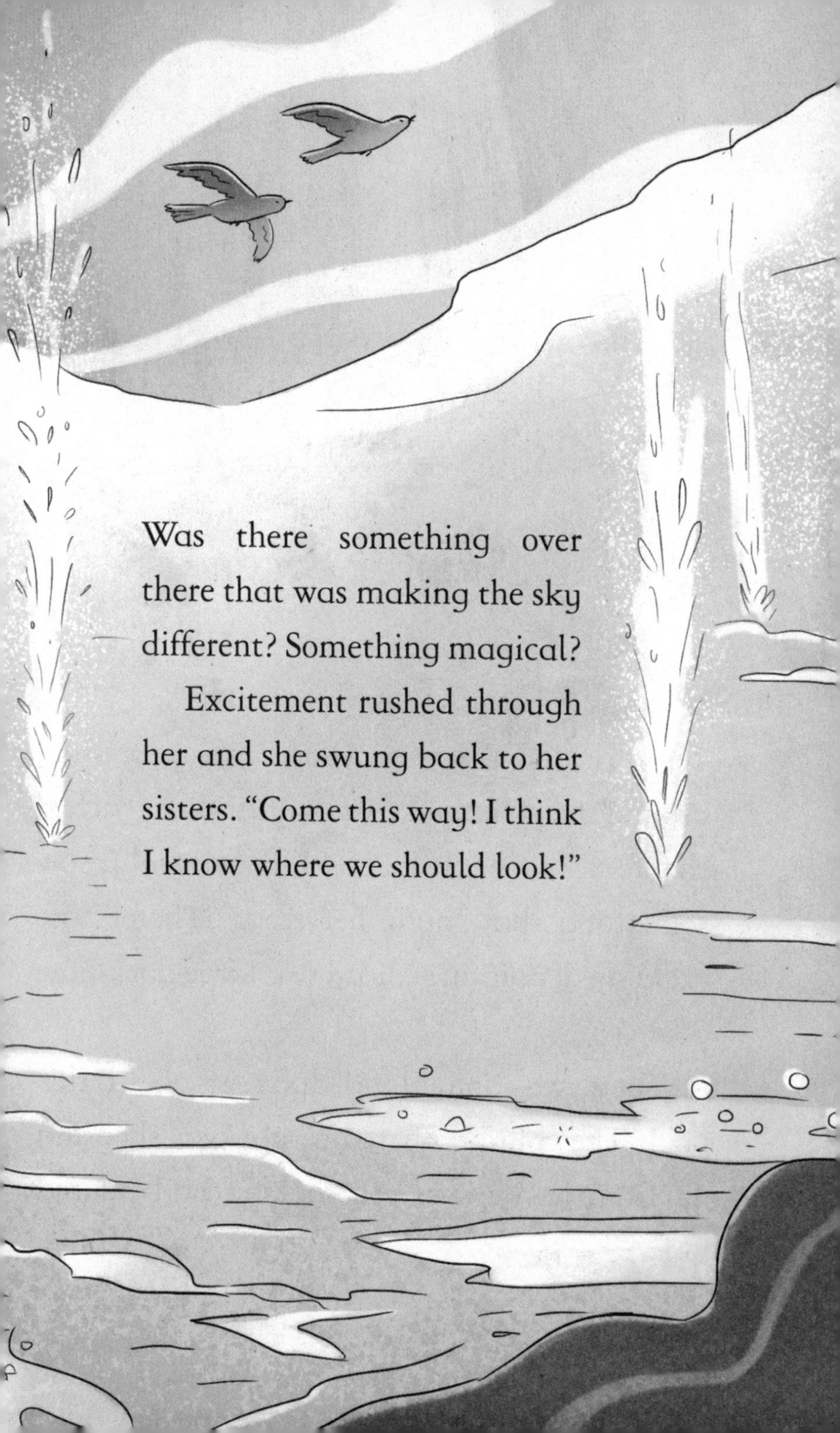

Was there something over there that was making the sky different? Something magical?

Excitement rushed through her and she swung back to her sisters. “Come this way! I think I know where we should look!”

Chapter Seven

The girls and Oskar edged their way carefully around the pools and craters until they reached the foot of the volcano. Ida suddenly saw something that made her stop. "There!" she exclaimed, pointing ahead to a large dark-blue pool.

There was something different about this pool. The column of steam that was shooting up from its depths into the sky had paused mid-eruption as if it had been frozen. The floating column of steam was glowing a dusky purple, and over the top of it arched a single perfect rainbow, frozen into place just like the steam. It was stunningly beautiful.

"The frozen rainbow," Hanna breathed, looking at the perfect rainbow glittering in the sun.

“The orb’s got to be hidden here!” said Magda in excitement.

“Let’s start looking!” said Ida. She thought of Aunt Veronika on the other side of the volcano and crouched down. “Oskar, please can you stay on guard for us?”

The cub knew what “on guard” meant. He gave a short chuff and pricked his ears as he turned to scan the surrounding geyser pits and craters.

“Perhaps the orb’s buried somewhere nearby,” Hanna suggested.

“There’s not much snow or earth,” Ida said, looking at the barren rocks around them. “It’s just lava with magma underneath.”

“Wait!” said Ida suddenly. “Look at the light—the purple light. It’s deeper at the top of the column, isn’t it?” The others followed her gaze and nodded as they saw she was right. At the top of the column, the light was dark purple, fading to lilac at the base where they were standing. "It could be because the orb is hidden at the top of the geyser—where the rainbow is," Ida said.

Hanna nodded. "But how are we going to get up there to find out?"

"Maybe I could draw something we could climb up? A ladder perhaps?" suggested Ida.

Just then Oskar gave a warning growl. They swung around and saw their aunt coming around the volcano with the lion. She gave an enraged shriek as she spotted them. "You girls!" she exclaimed, her voice carrying across the craters. "How did you escape?" Her eyes fell on the suspended geyser behind them. "The orb!" she breathed, looking up at the purple light.

Oskar growled fiercely and started to bound toward her.

"No, Oskar!" Magda cried.

But she was too late.

A ball of green light flew from her aunt's fingers and hit Oskar's chest. He gave a whimper and collapsed.

"What have you done to him?" screamed Magda.

"It'll be you next, nieces!" cackled the Shadow Witch.

She raised her hands to the skies and screeched out a command, then she pointed to the ground in front of her and made a snatching movement with her fingers. A stream of molten lava bubbled out of the ground, glowing yellow and red. The Shadow Witch brought her hands together and the magma turned into a huge blazing ball. She sent it rolling toward the girls like a bowling ball made of fire. Hanna grabbed Ida and Magda and pulled them out of the way just in time. It bounced over the rocks and hit

the wall of the volcano, exploding into molten pieces.

"Ow!" gasped Hanna as one of the pieces scorched her cheek.

Their aunt cackled and sent another two balls toward them.

The girls dodged them, but overhead the sky seemed to grow darker. Magda glanced up and saw a flock of ravens flying down at their heads, beaks and claws out, poised to attack. "Look out!" she cried to her sisters.

She flung herself to the side, only just avoiding another ball of magma. She tripped and fell, covering her head with her hands as a raven attacked her. Its sharp beak pecked at her fingers and her hair, making her yell.

"Leave my sister alone!" Hanna used her magic to send some of the ravens tumbling through the air. The birds squawked in panic

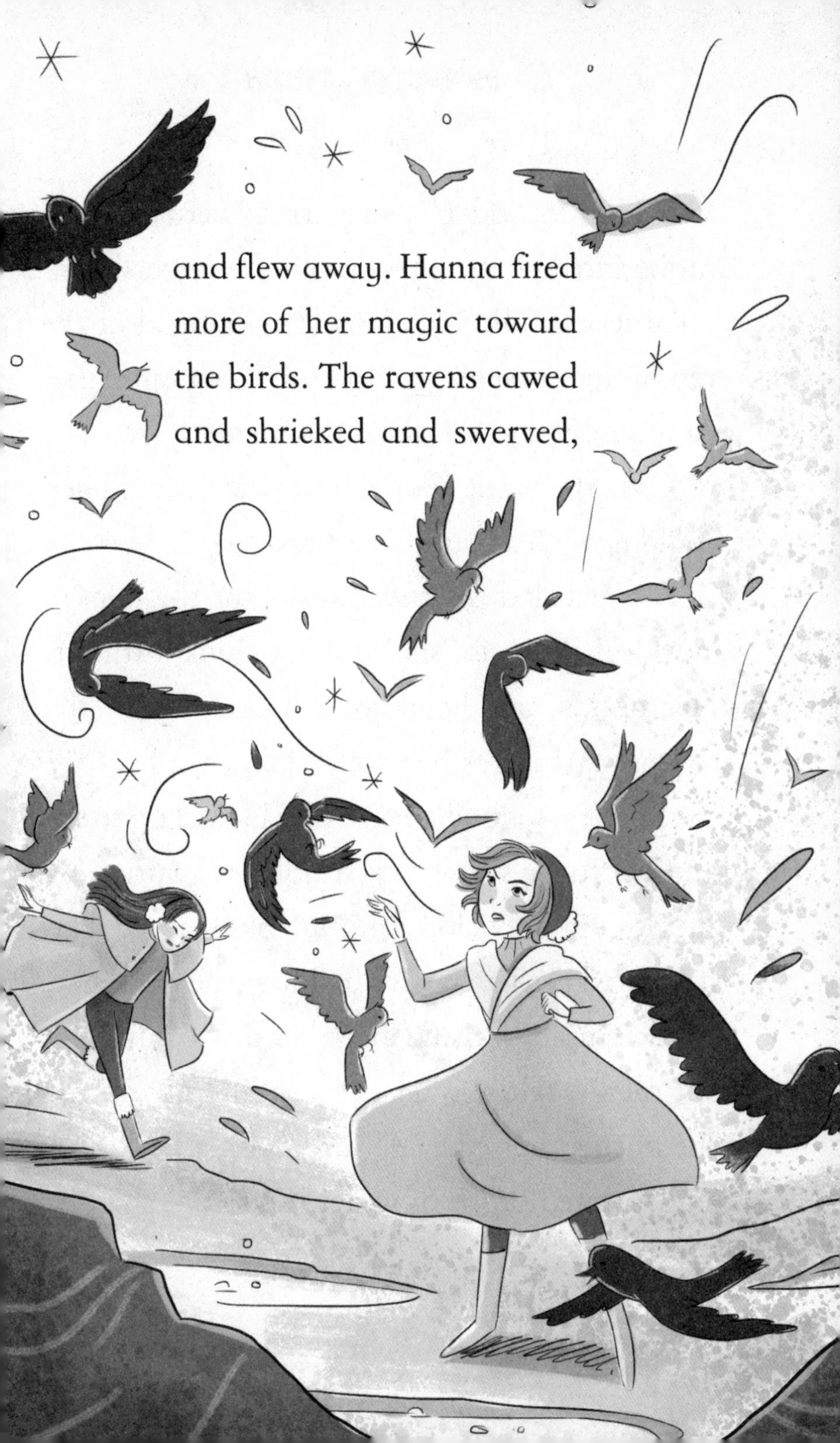

and flew away. Hanna fired more of her magic toward the birds. The ravens cawed and shrieked and swerved, and Hanna had to concentrate very hard to make sure her magic didn't hit her sisters.

Magda undid her cloak and charged at the remaining ravens, yelling and swinging her cloak around and fighting them off.

Over the cacophony of the raven's calls they could hear their aunt cackling.

Ida crawled around the side of the geyser. With all the noise she couldn't think straight. Her hands and head were hurting from the ravens' attack. What were they going to do? She heard a savage screech and looked up to see another raven swooping straight at her face, its eyes gleaming viciously. "No!" she gasped. She staggered backward and fell into the geyser.

Ida tensed, waiting for the steam to burn her, but all she felt was a gentle tingling warmth. She opened her eyes. All around her beautiful multicolored drops of water floated in the air.

She stared in wonder. Through the glittering curving sides she could just make out what was happening outside, as if she was looking through a window made of thick glass, but she couldn't hear anything. Inside the geyser was silent and peaceful, like being in an enchanted magical cave. She looked up and saw the purple orb floating far above her. If only she could get it, then maybe they could all somehow escape.

"Oh, I wish I could get to the orb," she said longingly.

She gasped as she felt herself rise a few centimeters off the ground. She was floating! But how was that possible? *Magic!* she realized. She felt a gentle pressure under her feet as the rainbow-colored steam started to push her up toward the orb.

Up and up she floated, through the multicolored drops of water, to where the orb was suspended at the very top of the geyser. As she got close, she could see purple light swirling through the delicate glass ball. She reached out, her fingers tingling as they closed around the orb.

"I've got it!" she breathed.

The magic slowly lowered her back to the ground. The second her feet touched down, the suspended water droplets start to shake. Instinct told her that the geyser wasn't going to stay frozen for very much longer. She had to get out!

With a gasp she flung herself at the wall. She fell through just as the geyser turned to steam again. She scrambled away to safety as the water splashed back down and the rainbow expanded and grew, covering the whole lava field with dazzling multicolored light.

The Shadow Witch staggered backward, shrieking, with her hands over her face as if the light was burning her eyes. The ravens flew off, squawking, and the lion roared and ran away. As the light hit Oskar, he shook his head and got to his feet, seemingly no worse for wear.

Ida saw her sisters staring at her in amazement. She scrambled to her feet and held the purple orb aloft. "I got it!" she cried. Magda and Hanna squealed in delight and ran over to her.

"No!" screamed the Shadow Witch, raising her hands.

Oskar snarled and bounded straight at her, growing into his full size. He butted her in the stomach with his head, sending her flying backward into a crater of thick mud. The Shadow Witch shrieked and thrashed around in the sticky, smelly blue-and-gray mud.

Oskar raced to the girls, his dark eyes shining proudly.

"Oh, well done, Oskar!" Magda cried. "And well done, Ida!"

"How did you get it?" Hanna demanded.

"I'll tell you when we're out of here," said Ida. "Let's go before Aunt Veronika escapes from the mud!"

They scrambled onto Oskar's back, Ida tucking the purple orb safely into her pocket.

"I said you wouldn't stop us, Aunt Veronika!" Ida shouted. "Now that we've got the orbs we're going to rescue Mother and Father and save Nordovia!"

Their aunt opened her mouth to shout back, but mud bubbled in. "I will get you for this!" she choked, spitting it out. "You will not thwart my plans!"

"Actually I think you'll find we just have!" Hanna grinned. She patted Oskar's neck. "Come on, boy, it's time to go home."

He leapt forward and carried the three girls across the treacherous lava fields and back to the safety of the castle.

Chapter Eight

"Girls!" Madame Olga's shriek was almost as loud and as terrifying as one of Aunt Veronika's as she hurried across the castle grounds toward them. The girls climbed wearily off Oskar's back. They had traveled home without stopping and were exhausted.

Oskar collapsed in a tired heap, shrinking back to his small size.

"We're in so much trouble," groaned Magda as Madame Olga steamed toward them. Her usual calm expression had been replaced by a look of fury.

Ida hid behind Hanna and Magda.

"Where have you been?" their governess demanded. "I got out of the shop to find the Shadow Witch had appeared and then you all go galloping off into the distance. Knocking over market stalls, causing chaos, stealing ponies—"

"Is Caspar, the pony, okay?" Magda interrupted. "Did he get back to the town?"

"Yes he did—he turned up at nightfall." Madame Olga wrung her hands together. "Girls, I have been beside myself with worry. Whatever possessed you to go off like that?"

"We had to," Magda said.

"Had to?" Madame Olga's eyebrows rose into her hairline. "Had to?"

"It was for Mother and Father . . ." Magda hesitated. They hadn't told anyone—not even Madame Olga—about trying to get the magical orbs. "We . . . er . . ."

"When we saw her at the market, we heard our aunt say something about where Mother and Father might be trapped, so we set off to try to find them," Hanna lied.

"And did you find your parents?" Madame Olga demanded.

The girls shook their heads.

Madame Olga looked at their filthy faces and tangled hair and the anger faded from her face. "Girls, girls, girls," she sighed, shaking her head. "I understand you want to find your parents, but you simply can't go running off like that, particularly not now your aunt is so close by. You must be more careful. Everyone in the palace is now on high alert. Please let the guards find your parents."

“We’re sorry, Madame Olga,” said Magda.

“We’re really tired and hungry,” said Ida.

“You look dreadful, and poor Oskar looks worn out,” said Madame Olga. “Take Oskar up to your room and put him in his bed and get changed. I shall ask cook to sort you out some food, even though I’m not sure you really deserve it.”

Ida could see the love behind her stern expression. “Thank you, Madame Olga,” she said.

"You're the best governess ever," said Hanna, smiling at her.

"Go on, off you go," said Madame Olga, shooing at them but looking very relieved.

Magda picked up Oskar and they headed into the castle. They all had the same thought—as soon as they got to their bedchamber they could put the purple lights into the snow globe.

The snow globe was on the table as usual, its snowflakes swirling endlessly around the waterfall that fell over the edge of a tall mountain into the icy sea.

Magda settled Oskar in his bed. He grumbled happily as he snuggled down in his soft blankets.

Ida took the purple orb out of her pocket. "Here we go!" she said, meeting her sisters' eyes.

They gathered around the globe.

Ida held the orb out and they all put their hands on it. As they moved it closer to the glass

of the snow globe the orb began to shine and sparkle.

They touched it to the glass and the orb vanished in a flash. They all gasped as blue, pink, and purple light met in an explosion of beautiful swirling color. And then an image of their mother's face appeared in the light. She looked pale but she was smiling.

"Mother!" cried Ida.

"You have done it!" Freya said weakly. "I can feel the Lights are back together. Oh, my clever, clever girls."

The triplets' hearts swelled with happiness.

"We found the purple orb by the frozen rainbow, just like you said," said Hanna.

"We had to fight Aunt Veronika," said Magda. "Oskar helped us."

"I am so proud of you." Their mother's emerald eyes shone with happy tears. "But there is one more challenge ahead. You must take the snow globe to the Silfur Falls—the highest waterfall in the land. Take it there on the Day of the Midnight Sun. If you fail and your aunt gets the snow globe, she will be able to harness the power of the Lights and become the ruler of Nordovia, bringing eternal darkness to the land. Be careful. She will do everything she can to stop you reaching the waterfall and take the globe from you."

"Where do we go when we get there?" Ida asked.

Their mother's face started to fade. "Watch!" she breathed. "The magic will show you." And then she was gone. The girls stared transfixed as the colorful lights in the globe swirled faster and faster and then vanished, and a line of silver, like a path, appeared, edging little by little along the cliffs to the top of the waterfall.

Then the silver path dived behind the waterfall and the scene lit up with a burst of bright pink, blue, and purple light.

The girls gasped as the waterfall turned

to shining silver, and the pink, blue, and purple lights were thrown up into the air. The strands of colored light twisted and danced in the globe just as they used to do in the Nordovian sky.

"The globe's showing us where we need to go," said Ida.

"And what we need to do," said Hanna. "We've got to put the Lights into the waterfall and then they'll return to the skies."

"And we'll have saved Nordovia," said Magda. "Mother will get her powers back and then she and Father will be free. Then they'll be able to celebrate the Day of the Midnight Sun with us."

"Do you think we can do it?" said Ida.

"I know we can!" Hanna declared.

Magda's eyes met her sisters'. "We have to," she said softly. "We can't fail."

They clasped one another's hands and gazed into the snow globe as the magical lights swirled on in a dance of hope above the silver waterfall.

The adventure continues in

THE ENCHANTED WATERFALL